Secrets
Behind the
Gates

Alma R. Nieves

Cover design by quality_world from Fiverr

Disclaimer: This is a fiction book. Some facts pertaining to
history and culture of Puerto Rico, Institutions, and dates
of natural disasters are mentioned, yet all the
circumstances, details and characters surrounding the facts
are fictional. Any resemblance to actual events or persons,
either living or dead, is entirely coincidental. The opinions
expressed are not those of the author, but of the characters.

Printed in the United States of America

1st Edition

For more information, contact the author at email
almanieves@ymail.com

Introduction

Storytelling is the social and cultural activity of sharing anecdotes. This art is sometimes complemented by improvisation, theatrics, poetry, or dance. Nearly every culture has its own form of storytelling. It is used as a form of entertainment, education, and cultural preservation. Many religions still use storytelling as a way to convey moral lessons as well. In ancient cultures, oral storytellers were regarded as healers, spiritual leaders, and teachers. They were known as the "cultural secret keepers." As it turns out, every place has its own secrets. It is an adventure and a mystery, not knowing if a story is true or how much of it is. Only the storyteller will ever know some things for sure, and other things… will remain secrets buried in our graves forever. This book is my way of sharing these stories and making them live on.

Chapter 1:

<u>Expectations</u>

It had never occurred to me what happens when a person dies. Everyone speaks of the spiritual aspect of that instant. Is there a soul? Does it go to Heaven? Maybe it travels south. Maybe it just wanders in this dimension, unseen by the human eye, watching, laughing, singing, or suffering, crying, desperate to find peace. Some people believe that a small percentage of humans have areas of their brains more developed than those of the majority, and these people can see or hear more. They see or hear the dead, some say. Raised in a Catholic family, I know all the prayers by heart. The debate of whether or not purgatory exists. You are never really sure who wins that one. We'll call it a huge maybe for now. That's one of those "I'll let you know when I die" kind of situations. How can you be really sure until you go through the experience? Who knows, right? Just like the concept of Hell, you picture it as a place with fire, demons, and maybe even a gondola crossing a sea of lost souls. That's not a coincidence. A famous European writer described it in his book "La Divina Comedia." Just like you picture it in your mind. He made the picture for us years back. He painted it, and our culture has accepted it, so now it just is the concept of Hell—thanks, Dante.

My degree was in marketing. The rhetoric in my mind stated that if you study hard and graduate, you will make something of yourself. I could still hear my father stating it. Your life would practically be designed according to the profession selected. Next, you would get married—to another professional, of course. One or two babies, maybe a cat or dog... and life would pretty much work itself out. You'd own a property or two. You'd travel and be a winner in this game of Life. You'd have attractive and intelligent children, you'd be able to pay for their college, and the cycle would go on. As the natural course of things should be.

Turns out that I got fired from my first extremely low-paying job by a 25-year-old southern white woman from the United States because I did not "participate enough in the meetings." I figured adulthood was just not as simple as my father said. It was in that July of 2017 that I realized I was 37 years old, fired by an incompetent child for no apparent reason, recently divorced, broke, about to have my apartment lease ended because they were selling the place, and just had no idea what my next move was going to be. To be honest, I did the only thing I had become a complete expert in doing while living in this colony called Puerto Rico, which seemed to be one chaos after the next: I decided to wing it.

I updated my resume and sent it to any email found on the internet regarding a job opportunity. I decided to take whatever job was available so that I could afford to at least move to a new place. I printed a few copies and went to any place that would take it, even if I secretly knew that it would be thrown in the trash. I kept driving to the next place and the next, and while lost in a rural route in Caguas on that Tuesday, July 13th, I stopped under a Flamboyán tree on the side of the road. It was full of blue flowers. I'd read that the blue Flamboyán exists, yet it's the rarest of its kind in Puerto Rico. We usually see red or yellow flowers, but I had never seen blue ones in person. The idea was to take some time to cry and complain about life, which, of course, I did. But the beauty of those blue flowers on that almost majestic tree kept catching my eye. And then I looked to my right and saw it—up next to the entrance to the oldest and largest cemetery in Puerto Rico: Flamboyán Memorial Park.

It had never occurred to me that there are people that work in funeral homes and cemeteries. You figure someone has to pick up the deceased, there's a process to be followed, and somehow the paperwork is filed, and the body winds up at a cemetery and is buried. But you never give thought to the actual people that get the job done—the people who deal with the crying, the yelling, the actual arrangement coordination that happens. The people who physically go in, dig those graves, and open them. I did not even want to drive in at first. So, I left my red Mazda 3 under the shadow of that rare Blue Flamboyán and walked to the entrance driveway.

It was a long-paved road, and, about half a mile in, two huge bronze gates stood. It looked like a custom design, with two Flamboyán trees, one on each side. As I came closer, holding my folder with the last copy of my resume, the gate automatically opened toward me. It felt as if I was walking into the promised land. There was a worker in a blue uniform. Young, maybe 23 or 24 years old, looking me dead in the eye. His name tag read Nelson.

As I came closer to the gate, he yelled, "We are closed. Union is on strike!"

I stopped in my tracks. I yelled back, "I just want to leave a resume in the office!"

He stared at the folder in my hand and said, "Make it quick. The other guys are having lunch, and no one should be coming in." I went in as quickly as I could and to the left of the gate, near the entrance, saw a small glass door that read "Oficina/Office." I pushed the door as it was open and left my resume on the front desk. There was no one there. Two weeks later, I received a call from the manager, Miguel Torres, for a phone interview. Turns out they were looking for a person to sell lots at the cemetery and arrange services for family members of the deceased. I never thought I would work at a place like that. He said I should report for work next Monday. *No paperwork. Just get here.* And that is how I wound up working at a cemetery. Never in my wildest dreams would I have thought I would be working there. It had never occurred to me before that moment. *I am an actual human being, and I will be working at a cemetery.*

Chapter 2:

Tita

Tita was a 30-year-old woman, thin, with a tattoo of a cartoon ant on her left forearm. Short, brown hair, huge red glasses. Too big for her face. Even though she was not tall, she was very outspoken and loud. She seemed intimidating, so I exchanged very few words with her in the first few days.

I was assigned a small cubicle right behind the front desk, and I spent all day hearing her conversations with the customers. She was loud. Always behind the reception desk, which was her fortress. I would listen to the daily conversations people had with her. I did not know that so many people visit cemeteries on a daily basis. Not only to schedule services but to make payments, ask questions, and look for tombstones of family members who had been buried. Tita was great at obtaining all the information—she was quick and efficient, making receipts while answering the phone and taking care of so many things at the same time. You could tell she had been working there for a while, yet she seemed bored. Constantly pissed off. Quick to respond in a defensive manner to the slightest tone or comment. She didn't care who it was. The attitude was present. Her motto was that the customer is right until he or she pisses her off. Maybe it was answering the same questions over and over every day that made her that way.

I noticed she always carried a notebook with her. Leather, medium-sized, black. She would write in it between customers. On my fourth day, I mustered the courage to sit at the same table she used in the lunch area. She gave me a glance and kept eating her lasagna. I asked if she was from the area and if she enjoyed writing, just to see if small talk was possible.

She said, "I've lived across from this cemetery my whole life. Sometimes I feel like I was born here. I write to stay alive in such a shitty world."

That's when I saw it. She was like a caged bird. A free soul forced to conform to a job so that she can afford to get by, yet never feel alive. I asked her, "Is that what you use that notebook for? Your poems or writing?"

She gave me a stern look and said, "No, this one is for my list of names." She showed me the notebook, which seemed small, yet it had over 200 pages. A smile took over her face. About half of the notebook had every line used with one word, front and back of the page. They were all the first names of deceased persons who were at that cemetery. It turns out that every time she spoke to a customer, she would look up the name of their deceased family member on the cemetery's computer. Her hobby was to write down every first name of the deceased in that notebook. She would also look up the death certificate to see what the cause of death was. She didn't write it down, though.

Curiosity got the best of me, and I looked through the list. There were some great interesting names: Agapito, Fredismunda, Aurora, and Wenceslao. She immediately sparked my curiosity. I went through the blank pages as well. The list seemed normal, with no particular order, just names, yet there was one peculiar thing. After the blank pages, on the last line on the very last page, it read "*Tita.*" I didn't dare to ask. She noticed what I saw. There was silence. I looked her in the eyes and smiled without saying a word. There was a look of kindness and understanding at that moment we shared. We became great friends.

Chapter 3:

<u>Ofelia</u>

F lamboyán Memorial Park was one of the largest and oldest cemeteries in Puerto Rico. Over 200 strings of land and about 50 strings were still undeveloped. I once counted ten field workers. You would always see them outside. Barely noticed them. Cutting grass, opening graves. There were 15-20 scheduled services daily. And they always got the job done. Quiet. The man who operated the digger was the oldest: 72 years old and still working. He knew every corner of that cemetery. He hopped on that digger in the morning and just sat on it until it was time to leave. He even had his lunch delivered by the cafeteria about a block away and ate it while still sitting up there. His name was Emilio. He had been working there since the cemetery was opened. No one talked about the cemetery's history.

One day, while I was lost searching for one of the lots, Emilio drove by and stopped. He asked, "Nena,

¿te ayudo?" (Girl, can I help you?) And not only did he help me that day, but he told me a little bit about where I was working. The cemetery was opened in 1961 and was owned by a Catholic Spaniard in the beginning. The years went by, and it was sold to an American company, as most of the businesses that operate in Puerto Rico were. Their benefits were reduced once these changes occurred, and they decided to participate in a Union. They rarely spoke to any of the employees in the office. But that day, he asked me to do him a favor—take his ATM Card and make a withdrawal at a teller nearby. It turns out that Emilio knew a lot of things, but he didn't know how to read. I did what he asked, and he thanked me for my help. He said I was the first "office person" to ever help a field worker. I laughed. He made it sound like "office people" were so different from his kind. The man couldn't read, but he knew a lot. He was the only expert in that cemetery. An expert in knowing the land, if water ran in a current under what we saw, what graves were harder or easier to open, how many deceased really fit in each burial space, and the list went on. Whenever there was a problem, Emilio was the one to figure the solution out.

Once you passed the massive gates at the entrance, to the left was the glass office door. Once inside, after passing the front desk and my assigned work area, there was a large staircase. The building had three floors. Tita and I were downstairs, and there were two more sales representatives: Jose, a 40-year-old bald man, not attractive yet very charismatic and loud, and Angela, a 62-year-old woman who had gray, short hair and always wore beads around her neck and in bracelets. They looked like wood. I heard the administration workers once commenting that she was Santera or some kind of African religion. She was from Jamaica and spoke Spanish with a thick accent. On the second floor, there were seven administration employees who rarely spoke to anyone other than themselves and the manager, Miguel. The administration employees, all women, all visited the same church. Overhearing their conversations, I found out that they even participated in a choir. It was like an exclusive club. Other than religious things, their only other topic was to talk about anyone who was not part of their "club." For example, the employees on the first floor. Once, while I was going up to the third floor, which is where all the cemetery files were located, I overheard them criticizing Tita's tattoos and how she would burn in Hell for desecrating her body.

I stood at the entrance of the second floor before continuing, and everyone automatically shut up and looked down. You could sense the awkward and uncomfortable situation. Except for Suzy. She was the oldest of the group, with long hair, always wearing a long jean skirt. She stared me blankly in the eye. I said, "Good afternoon," and she continued to stare silently. She did not speak to people outside of her group and was very obvious about it. She believed and verbalized that she possessed God's light. Yet, secretly, nobody really liked her. I kept moving. I could feel the hate in her stare.

As I continued to the third floor that day, there was the file room. The cemetery had over 25,000 lots, and every single one of those lots had a file. There was that entire third floor, full of wood shelves for all those files. From A-1 to Z-696 in the first section, then AB-1 to AZ-1, and the sections went on and on. When you walked into the file floor, you could smell how old the papers were. I can best describe it as a dusty, moldy smell. At the end of the room, there were large metal drawers. In them were very large books. All handwritten. They were the records of the names of all the deceased names with the plots where they were buried. On the outside of each book, there were years written. There was one book from 1961 to 2023, all identified. All the burials were documented by hand in those leather books.

On my first day at that cemetery, I was going through the book from 1963, just curious to see the person's handwriting and how things were documented at that time when suddenly, the lights went out. I turned on my phone flashlight and found the light switch was to the left of the metal drawers. I flipped it, and the lights came back on. I went back to the open drawer and looked down once again at the book, and "click," the lights went off again.

"Hm," I grabbed my phone once again from my pocket. And right at that moment, it seemed like I was hearing humming. It was coming from the first section of files, near the exit to the stairs, or at least it seemed like it. It sounded like the singing voice of an older lady. *Was I hearing this right, or was my mind playing tricks on me?* I thought. ¿Oubao Moin? That's a poem written by Juan Antonio Corretjer and later made a song by Roy Brown. My grandfather would sing it, and I knew that melody by heart. I looked over at the switch with my flashlight, and it was down as if someone had turned it off. That's when I felt a cold chill run down my spine. I decided to flip the switch again, and the lights came on. I quickly placed the book in the drawer, left it half open, and went straight for the stairs. I could still feel goosebumps from that chill that ran through my spine. As I went by that first section of files: *silence.* I placed my foot on the first step to go down the stairs and "click." The lights were off again. I got out of there.

I quickly paced down the stairs to my cubicle, still kind of jumpy. When Angela saw me, she asked me where I had been, and I said, "On the third floor," still trying to shake the goosebumps off my arms. She grinned, almost about to burst out laughing, and said, "I see you met Ofelia. You look a little pale."

16

Chapter 4:

<u>Don Sergio</u>

One Monday, there was a very old man searching grave by grave in one of the sections of the cemetery. White guayabera shirt, tan pants, black moccasin shoes. He had a hat on his head. He had a very old envelope in his hands with papers that looked yellow, as though they were just as old as he was. I saw him in the morning and in the evening, still searching. As I drove by in one of the golf carts, taking another family to a grave, I stopped to see if he needed help. He was very angry and started crying and yelling. He said he had bought a lot in 1987 and the papers in his envelope were so old they couldn't be read anymore. He had gone to the office, and Angela had told him there was no record of his purchase and that since the papers were not legible, he had to purchase another lot. His wife was bedridden, and he was preparing everything for when she passed. He had no money for a new lot because he had spent all their savings on her care. I felt my chest get tight. I told him to sit in his car and wait, asked for his information, and went up to the file room.

I searched all the files in the area where he was and couldn't find anything under his name. As I was sitting on the floor, I heard some files fall from a section about two rows down from where I was sitting. There was no one there. I got up to place them back and felt a gust of cold wind. There were no windows in the file room. I placed the files back and went off to see Don Sergio, who I had told to wait in his car. He was smiling when I came back, but I wasn't. I couldn't find the file for his purchase.

There I was, standing under the sun with Don Sergio and his worry, and I felt the noise of the digger coming to my right. Emilio stops and sticks his head out the side to yell, "¿Te ayudo?" (Can I help you?) He told me he remembered having seen this man but didn't know his name. He says in the '80s, there were problems with some large stones in the area, and those lots had to be moved. "Dile que me siga" (Tell him to follow me). I did too. We both followed him. He got to a very small section near the back part of the cemetery. All the graves had tombstones. He pointed to one of the lines. And there it was. Three plots from the road, his last name on the tombstone. I couldn't believe it myself. Don Sergio cried in relief. I wrote down the plot number on my hand and went back to the file room to get the old man the evidence he needed. I went back up to the third floor and straight to the area where those letters and numbers were. Shit, it was the file that had fallen on the floor. No one knows this place better than Emilio and Ofelia.

Chapter 5:

<u>Maria</u>

We were used to hurricanes living on an island. The natives that first populated this island, according to our history books, were the Taino Indians. We were taught that they were peaceful, except when fighting the Caribe Indians, who were our cannibalistic neighbors. They had many gods (or deities, as they are also called) who they worshiped. Guabanex was one of the most respected. It was assumed that she was a woman, although we were not sure of that fact. Truth be told, we didn't know much about the Taíno population. Now, what was known was that Guabanex controlled the weather. Most of the time, it was a little rain every now and then and sunny most of the time. But every so often, she spawned the wind and decided to create chaos by releasing the Zemi (Cemí, in Spanish) or deity named Juracán. That is where the word Huracán and Hurricane comes from. The fact of the matter is you do not want to mess with Guabanex.

I lived through numerous hurricanes while living in Puerto Rico. It's a tropical island near the Equator. I'd say it's just part of the package. When I was just a toddler, in 1989, Hurricane Hugo passed. I don't remember much except darkness and a particular howling sound that the wind made. I was little, so I can't recall much of that one. Of the bigger ones I remembered was Georges in 1998. Not because of the wind, in particular, but because of the floods. My grandparents lived near a lake, and it rained so much that they had their house flooded to about three feet. Everything in the home was lost. As Puerto Ricans, we stick together when a hurricane hits and try to be in the same household with as many family members as possible. I remember my grandpa heading out with a machete when the water started coming into the house, trying to get the trunks and fallen leaves out of the city sewer transport right in front of the house, but it was too much. So he headed inside, and he held my grandmother, my two brothers, and me on the bed, and we waited. My parents were in the next room on top of another bed, and what I remember most was my grandmother's voice while praying el Santo Rosario nonstop for the next close to eight hours. She didn't stop. She knew the Virgin Mary would protect us. And she always did.

In a few hours, the rain started to cease, and the water went down. This was probably the day in my life when I learned that all things are replaceable. We were just happy that we were all ok. I remember we spent about a week and a half with no electric power. We played cards and dominos and had a small gas camping stove where grandma kept cooking. Everything we needed was there. I miss my grandparents. I kept my grandfather's machete and my grandmother's rosary. May they rest in peace.

We had a few more hurricanes here and there, but nothing too bad. Now on September 16, 2017, Hurricane Maria hit. Category 4 winds over 250 kilometers per hour. It had been over 100 years since a hurricane of that magnitude had passed through our island. We had our supplies set, but no one could be ready for something like that. All you could hear was the wind, this deafening howling and destruction. Trees falling, palm trees, cars being crushed by them, glass breaking, the Guacamayo parrots trying to find shelter in any open corner of the homes, and water. There was water everywhere. I lived in a place called Levittown at the time; it was near one of the largest water dams on the island. Luckily, the apartment I leased was at the bottom of a two-story house that had outside stair access.

By hour five, the water dam was too full, and with no warning, someone (probably some clueless politician) gave the order to open the gates and have the water run out while it was still raining and the wind was at its maximum. The water started rushing uncontrollably into all the houses. I saw the water level rising, took my grandmother's rosary, twisted it around my wrist, and decided to get out. I couldn't get the front door open because the water kept pushing it shut. I looked at the window to the right of the door. It was old, one of those aluminum sheet windows. The water was already at the bottom sheet. I had no time to waste. I kicked the next aluminum sheet out and the next, and I was able to fit my body through that hole and get out. I still have no idea where my strength came from. As I got out, I would just continue to hear the wind and screaming. I couldn't tell where it was coming from exactly. More than one house. I kept my back against the outside wall of the house as I slid sideways to get to the stairs. The water was already getting to my chest. I grabbed the metal rail on the stairs and ran up as fast as I could. I had to wait in front of my upstairs neighbor's door until the wind stopped. It felt like days. I prayed to the rosary nonstop until the wind calmed down a bit.

Two days of darkness. I wasn't sure if I was dreaming or awake, but I heard a helicopter in the distance. It was still dark; you couldn't tell what time of the day it was. The one-story houses in the street were completely underwater. I could only see the cement rooftops that remained. The helicopter landed on a neighbor's roof, and they had a loudspeaker. They were searching for survivors. The rain had not stopped, so they hurried out. I don't know if my neighbor was in her apartment or not, but the door never opened. I was frozen, with my head buried between my knees, praying. I didn't want to see what was around me. I could hear the helicopters traveling back and forth and trying to get people out of their homes. At least a few were able to make it to their roofs, and I heard them calling for help. As the water level went down, night fell. I was able to go back to my apartment. Mud and water everywhere. I couldn't speak. I just sat until the sun rose on day three as if Hell had not just broken loose on our island.

I opened the door. *Emergency personnel should be arriving at any moment*, I thought. Most of the people who drowned were elders who just could not make it to the top of their roofs. It was complicated to access the street because there were tree trunks blocking the access and rubble everywhere. I heard some of the neighbors yelling that they had gas chainsaws. I grabbed my grandfather's machete from what was left in the mud of the closet and went out to help. There was a huge tree blocking the access to our street. Everyone that had a chainsaw or machete climbed that huge log and went at it. We needed people to be able to access the road so help could arrive. I had never used that machete, and this was the perfect time to learn. We chopped and chopped at one of the sides until we were able to make a small way through. All of the light posts were on the ground or tilted completely sideways, and power cords were on the ground. My upstairs neighbor finally appeared. She had a large carbon grill upstairs. She was telling all the neighbors to bring their meats so they wouldn't rot in the refrigerators, and we made a barbecue for the survivors on the street. We sat and ate and wondered. Help should arrive soon. Nightfall again. No one came.

The next morning, I decided to walk with one of my neighbors. We had to get out when the noon sun hit the rooftops of the homes on our one-way street—an unforgettable smell took over. I can't make a fair comparison for this one... the smell is death. There were some houses where the doors had not reopened, and no one dared to enter. So, we walked in search of help. There was no electric power, most roads were still blocked by trees, and there were people trying to make way. Whoever was able to save their cell phone said there was no service. A few streets down was Tito's gas station. There was a long line of people standing outside. I could hear Tito yelling, "Ya no hay hielo, ¡¡no hay gasolina!!" The faces of the people in line were almost gray. No feeling. A few were talking about all the damage to their homes and what we were all to do next. In that line, I saw an older man, maybe 80 years old, with a battery-operated radio and came closer to hear. The signal wasn't good, with a lot of static, but I could make out that it was one of the local radio stations. Family members were calling from outside of Puerto Rico to check if their loved ones had survived. There was no cell phone signal; the phone signal towers had all fallen. I kept walking toward my mother's home, which was a few blocks down. One of her cars wasn't in the driveway. My neighbor had a pen and napkin in her bag, so I left her a note saying I was ok and walked back. I noticed people on the sides of the roads in their cars trying to get a cell phone signal. Nothing.

When I passed the gas station again, I noticed the old man still listening to his radio. He was in line while sitting in a beach chair. I went by him again and asked him, "Do you happen to have a landline at home?"

"¡Pues claro!" (Of course!) He pointed us to his house. Three houses down and then a right. Clara esta allí. Just tell her Negrón sent you." And so, we arrived at Doña Clara's house.

Chapter 6:

<u>Clara</u>

A t Doña Clara's house, they had food and water. She had made un sopón as if she was expecting company. We ate and told her what had happened on our street. She gave us some of her daughter's clothes because she lived in the United States, and it had been years since she had been back. Luckily, she had kept them in a large plastic bin that was safe from the rain. Clara had to be about 73 years old, but no one dared to ask her age. You never ask a Puerto Rican woman her age. We were telling her about what happened in our block, and she looked down at the rosary in my hand. "La Virgencita te protegió Nena." She knew the Virgin Mary had protected me.

Clara was short, with tan skin and many wrinkles. Her hair was short, completely white, no glasses. Her smile was endearing. Even though it was a bit crooked, she smiled, and it brought peace to everyone near her.

She cooked for whoever came over to eat. Doña Clara didn't have much in her home. Her daughter lived in the United States, and she had no grandchildren. The house was cement, but the roof was zinc plates, so the hurricane destroyed it. Negrón had bought a tarp at the gasoline station and set it up to cover the house and the few things remaining from the rain. He also brought two packs of white rice and two cans of tuna. "Come back whenever you are hungry," they said, and we did for the next four days.

I still have no idea how Doña Clara did it. But she fed everyone who came through that door with her sopón, two bags of rice, and two tuna cans for the next four days, at least. It was like she multiplied the food. I saw random people entering and leaving her home, helping her clean the house and eating. Some brought materials to rebuild the roof and, in a few days, had at least half of the roof done. The tarp covered the other half. And Doña Clara kept cooking and feeding people and never felt lacking in anything. She would hug everyone and give each their "bendición" on the way out... and then you were family. The woman kept no record of what she gave and always received. It was beautiful to meet such an amazing human. I hope to be like Doña Clara when I grow up.

Chapter 7:

The rescue team

It was day five, and we still had no running water. I was trying to clean some of the mess and mud but couldn't do much. It had all dried, and with no running water, it was an impossible task. In the clothes Clara gave me, there was a pair of jeans, socks, underwear, and some t-shirts. I was just happy to be able to wear clean clothes. Finally, the sounds of machinery and workers could be heard clearing the way. Military personnel arrived in three huge vans supplying water and food packs. The third vehicle had no supplies. It looked like a large, refrigerated trailer. The men asked if there were any missing neighbors and went to those homes. The smell really took over that day. They took down the doors of the unopened homes and placed the bags, one on top of the other, in the refrigerated container. The man driving the van wrote on a list he had on a writing pad. No one asked. We just stood looking through our open doors and windows as the men worked. I had never realized how much one could say when standing in complete silence. The men's faces were emotionless. Tears went down my face as reality hit me. I wasn't dreaming.

I had lost my sense of time and realized I had to find a way to get back to work. Everything was lost in my home. I had to ensure the income to replace things and get at least part of my life back. This place was for sale anyway, so I had to move. I just didn't know I would be starting from scratch. I asked one of the men his name and in what direction they were headed. Ben was his name, and he said they were about done for the day. Ben was from the United States. He had been sent from Nashville, Tennessee, to assist in the rescue efforts in Puerto Rico and other "classified" missions here—whatever that means. He said if I kept it quiet, they could give me a ride to San Juan. I got in and didn't think about it. With a bottle of water and the clothes on my back, I headed to wherever they were taking me. I sat in the back of the first truck, between a few of the water cases that were left. Once at San Juan, I thanked the guys and took a few food packs for the way. I had to walk for about three hours. It got cold and windy as the sun set on the mountains. And I was finally there. Flamboyán Memorial Park. The gate was closed, and night had fallen. I had no clue what time it had been for the last five days. I sat with my back against the gate and slept. Enjoyed the peace the cemetery brought. As I felt the sun rising and the light on my skin, I noticed that I felt warm. When I woke up and came to my senses, I noticed a blanket covering me. I must have been so tired not to notice that someone had come to place it on me. I still wonder who and how it got there. What I know for sure is that I slept nice and warm that night thanks to that good Samaritan.

Emilio was always the first person to arrive at the cemetery—5:00 a.m. sharp every day, seven days a week. The sun still had not risen, and he was having breakfast in the parking lot. Then, Nelson got there. He was the Union representative and was always aware of the needs of the field workers. I saw him a few times in the office having heated discussions with the manager about their work conditions. I never paid too much attention, though. I wasn't part of the Union, so it was really none of my business.

When I walked in with the blanket still on me, they were ready with breakfast for me. Coffee and toast. Nelson says, "Emilio tells me you are part of the family. We got you." And they did. Nelson even lent me his car and a sofa to sleep on in his home while I got a new place to live. Turns out you are safe when you are family with these guys. It was a good feeling.

Chapter 8:

El Santo Rosario

I kept my grandma's rosary on my right wrist all the time. Even though I had to replace my things little by little, I felt safe no matter where I slept or what was happening around me. I am not sure how many days had gone by, maybe two. The only people at the cemetery who could get to work so far were Emilio, Nelson, the manager Miguel, and me. Since Flamboyán Memorial was the largest cemetery in Puerto Rico, it also had a huge crematorium. We were operating with what was left of the diesel for the power plant and a partial roof on that building. Luckily, the huge ovens inside had remained intact through all the destruction the hurricane brought. There were five ovens. Emilio knew how to operate them, so he explained the steps, and Nelson and I followed.

We rarely saw Miguel on those days. I went back to the office to rest sometimes and saw him with his elbows on his desk and his head buried in his hands.

His eyes seemed lost. So, I went back to the crematorium and kept working.

Some ovens were older than others. Since the crematorium personnel had not come back to work and the phone lines were still not operating, anyone with available hands was receiving the bodies of the deceased at the crematorium as they arrived. Some in funeral hearses, some in those refrigerated trailers the military men were driving. There were so many bodies received the following days. We didn't count. We didn't think. We didn't check the permits. We just worked.

There was a small radio in the crematorium, which was battery-operated. It was small and old; it had a very long metal antenna which had to be located close to one of the windows to get a signal. The radio was kept on so we could hear what was going on outside while we worked: The President of the United States stated that there were three reported dead in Puerto Rico with Hurricane Maria's passing... 4... 6. We looked at each other and said nothing. It took three to four hours to cremate most human remains, so the sitting in silence was long.

We took notes in the logs of the crematorium, number, permit, and plastic urn and kept going. There was a large refrigerator at the back, which we had to turn off in order to keep the ovens going with the diesel that was left. So many roads were still blocked, and we had no idea when we would be able to get more diesel to keep operating. I noticed there was one body in a wood casket still in the refrigerator. With the days that had passed, the smell was becoming unbearable. Nelson told Emilio that we should have that body cremated as well. Nelson opened the refrigerator and went in with his shirt covering his nose and mouth to see how heavy the wooden casket was. A tag at the bottom read his name, "Abimael Bravo," and the word "Judio."

My conscience would not allow me to cremate a Jewish person. Although my grandmother was Catholic, she had Jewish descendants in Europe, so I knew they should be buried in the ground. I explained this to Emilio, and he said he would be right back. He left the crematorium walking and said nothing else. About 35 minutes later, he arrived back on the digger. He proceeded to open an empty grave near the crematorium building. First with the digger and then finished with the shovel he always carried with him in the machine. The container was heavy, so we needed help. Nelson was strong but very thin, and I wasn't exactly a weightlifter or gym buff, so we wanted to avoid getting hurt. No medical attention would be available for a while.

I went down to the office in the golf cart and told Miguel to stop crying and get in. He was sitting behind the reception desk at that moment and did as I said.

While driving up to the crematorium again, he asked me how we could work at a time like this. I told him "in silence" was the best way. We got in there, and Miguel asked no questions. I told him to help us lift the casket and place it on a metal cart Nelson had already prepared. That smell. It never leaves your memory once you've experienced it. Once on the cart, we pushed the container out to the grave Emilio had opened. With belts Emilio had (also on the digger), we tied the sides of the container and carefully placed it in the ground.

Emilio was ready to close the grave with the digger, and I asked him to wait a minute. I took my grandmother's rosary and started praying, "Padre Nuestro que estas en el Cielo, santificado sea tu Nombre, venga a nosotros tu Reino." I asked Abimael to forgive me because I knew he was Jewish, but I was doing my best. There was a loud sound, like something hitting wood very hard. We looked at each other and then again, twice more. The smell became unbearable. We looked in the grave, and the container had burst. Emilio immediately turned on the digger to close the grave. I stood to watch the soil cover what was left of the container. Abimael deserved to be accompanied at this moment, no matter the circumstances. I kept praying. Luis and Nelson went inside the building because they could not tolerate the smell, but I was so concentrated I hardly noticed anymore.

The grave was completely closed, and Emilio got down from the digger and put his arm around me in a hug. It was the first time I cried. *Rest in peace, Abimael. We've got you covered.* I remembered my grandmother's voice in my head saying, "A quien obra bien, le va bien." (Whoever does good will do well). I guess that my grandmother became my conscience after she died. It's a strange feeling how someone can be not physically present but never leaves you.

Then, Tita's Blue Corolla honked. She had made her way back to work and didn't find anyone at the office. I immediately felt relief as I looked up and saw her. Things would be back to normal little by little. Emilio walked away and back to the crematorium to keep working. Work, work, work.

Chapter 9:

Ghosts

The cemetery employees had little contact with workers in the funeral homes. Sometimes, when the family needed assistance in purchasing a property for burial, they would call the cemetery, and we would have to drive over to that funeral home to get all the paperwork done for the service. Since there were three salespeople at Flamboyán Memorial Park, we would take turns as to who had to drive over that day. After that, we would see the employee again when they would drive the funeral hearse to the cemetery on the day of that family's service. I was told some great ghost stories about things that had happened in the different funeral homes. I figured people just have a wild imagination.

It was a Thursday afternoon, and the call came in to visit one of the funeral homes to help a family with their service. It was my turn. I was just about to head out from my shift but decided to be nice and visit the funeral home on my way out to have everything set for that family. One of their sons had died suddenly. The cause of death was still not known, but they had to have arrangements in order to be able to proceed with the burial. I didn't have the heart to make them wait. Luckily, that particular funeral home was just five minutes away from the cemetery and right on my way home.

As I parked my new blue Toyota Yaris in the parking lot, I stopped for a second to look at the sunset. The sky looked like it was painted orange. It was always nice to have a small pause during the day and look at something beautiful, especially when you deal with death and grief all day.

Once I headed inside, I met with the funeral attendant and the family and got to work. There were no viewings on that Thursday, which was uncommon because that was one of the most popular funeral homes on the island. As I was finishing up the paperwork, I could hear a child's laughter in the hallway, right outside the conference room we were in. I figured the family probably had more than one child, and since there were no services that day, I kept working on the paperwork with the family there with me. A few seconds later, I could hear the laughing and run again. The mother that was with me had to be about 30 years old. She was visibly heartbroken, and you could tell she had been crying all day.

The father was serious and cold, his eyes fixed on the table, not looking up the entire time we were there. He was probably a few years older than her. He had gray hair. He looked up at me and asked, "They let you bring your kids here?" I told him I didn't have kids and stood up to go check.

As I left the conference room and passed a small reception desk, I saw a kid run right past me. Maybe six, at the most. He had a yellow suit on. I looked back at the funeral attendant, who was in an office right behind me, and asked, "Who is that child?" He didn't pay much attention, looked up, and shrugged. I looked back to where the child was running and couldn't see him. Yet I still heard his laugh from a distance.

"Pepe, can you hear the laughter?"

He replied: "Yeah… don't worry."

I went back to the family and quickly finished the paperwork, then walked them to the parking lot. I never went to that funeral home after work again. It had been one year working at the cemetery, and it was the second time I felt that chill down my spine. You don't get used to some things.

Two days later, I again met the family for the cemetery service. They had balloons in the shape of cars, and all the flower arrangements were made of sunflowers. Two vehicles were just for flowers and toys, and one for the casket.

As I led them to the graveside, I had to quiet my mind. *Don't think about it, Vero*. I knew they had lost a child. It turns out he had a brain tumor. The tumor was so aggressive that the child only lasted weeks once diagnosed. Six years old. I parked the golf cart used to lead the families to the graves and began moving the flowers and balloons. The father greeted me and asked me to be quick. They had already done their service and prayers at the funeral home; they did not want to keep extending the pain. The family members began to park their vehicles on the side of the road near the grave and walked over.

Nelson and Juan, another field worker, had placed wood planks over the grave to hold the casket while the family said their last goodbyes. As Juan opened the door to the funeral vehicle, I heard the father's shout. "I'll do it." He came right to the hearse. He rolled out his son's casket, paused, and lifted it. The casket was wood and small; he was able to comfortably lift it from the vehicle. Without thinking, he placed the casket on the wood planks above the opened grave. The mother and the older sister (maybe seven or eight years old, at the most) were gently sobbing on the right side of the grave. I stood near them, looked up, and saw Emilio on the digger. We shared a glance. There were no words.

Nelson was in a hurry, and there were still four more services to go that day. He bluntly asked, "Ya? We ready?" I gave him a stern stare. He stepped back and looked at Emilio on the digger, who nodded his head. "La Nena nos dice" (the girl will say). Nelson was not happy, but he would always do as Emilio said. He stepped away and stood next to Juan. I instructed the family to release the balloons, and they did, as I removed sunflowers from the floral arrangements to give to the family members. I asked Juan and Nelson to proceed once the family nodded in agreement.

Juan climbed inside the grave and asked Nelson to hand him the casket. As they were placing him, I could only hear the mother's screaming. Once Juan climbed out of the grave with Nelson's help, I asked the family members to toss the sunflowers inside the grave. It looked like a yellow blanket covering that small casket in the dirt. I looked up at Emilio and asked the family to step back. Emilio turned on the digger and began closing the grave with the mountain of dirt right beside it. The mother dropped to her knees and kept screaming and crying, the father and other daughter hugging her on the ground. It was the sound of living the worst pain you can experience in a lifetime. My eyes watered. Juan and Nelson were no longer in a rush. The funeral vehicle began to leave, and the mother kept screaming and crying. I offered her water, but she couldn't stop. She just looked up and me and asked if she was awake. I couldn't hold my tears back. That was not regular grief—the one you get used to working at a cemetery every day. It was human nature that called me to hug a complete stranger. Because life is just unfair sometimes, and boy, was it unfair to them on that day. There's no consolation for that. I don't think they will ever be the same again.

As Emilio finished closing the grave with the digger, the family members began to leave. The mother stayed. I placed the remaining flowers on the closed grave and said goodbye. Her eyes were like glass, and she was standing now, just staring at the ground with no emotion. The father said, Thank you," and I was on my way. Losing a child is probably the worst pain a human being can endure. It's just the interference of the natural order of things... Your elders, well, it's sad but a different kind of grief. But to lose a child. I mean, the body is just not biologically prepared for it. I had pain in my chest all day after that. I had to leave work early because I just couldn't stop thinking about how unfair life had been to that family. I was not even sure if I would go back to work the next day.

A few days later, the child's father came by the cemetery to say thank you and gave me one of the prayer cards from his boy's service. It was thin cardboard, small, simple. There was a small picture above the prayer that read below. The picture was of his smiling, happy boy... and he was wearing a yellow suit.

Chapter 10:

<u>Secrets</u>

S aturday was always a terrible day to work at the cemetery. The field workers were off, and there was only one administration worker per shift. Very rarely did Miguel come in on a Saturday. But the salespeople, we had to be there, and Tita had to cover reception, no matter what. Even though she was part of the administration group, there were different rules for her. Everyone else called in sick that Saturday, and I was the only salesperson there. Tita was rushing with people coming to request information to visit their families' gravesides at reception, and Susana was doing her online shopping on her phone on the second floor. We called her extension, no answer. Since it was an older cemetery, a lot of information was not on the computer, and you had to go to the books and files to gather information. We did our best, as usual.

The manager, Miguel, had been transferred about a year ago from a different cemetery the company owned. Rumor had it that his assistant, who also happened to be Suzy's sister, was his lover and had a child out of wedlock with him. They were both married. Tita told me that he had been separated from his wife since then due to the problems caused by this situation. Suzy's sister, Gwendolyn, had left her husband in hopes that Miguel would propose marriage. She was pretty upset when he decided he was confused about his feelings and wanted to work things out with his wife. So much so that she made a scene at Human Resources, claiming sexual harassment, and he was transferred within a few days to a different work location. Now, he had to drive about an hour and a half to work and pay child support. Miguel Padro was always quiet—he had a heavy energy about him. It was almost sad to sit near him for a long period of time. His office was on the first floor, behind the reception desk, but there were always piles of files and paperwork. He was never there. He either worked from his car or, on the days Suzy was there, at a desk next to her. Angry people would often request to see the manager, but he was never available. Sometimes he would walk past a customer yelling at Tita at the reception desk, and he would almost go by unnoticed. No one knew or thought he was the manager. I had noticed his black Audi that Saturday at the cemetery since I arrived, yet there was no sign of him. I kept working.

It was 3 p.m., and Tita and I were exhausted. We had spent the entire day dealing with angry customers because they had to wait in line. There were only two of us, yet people expected miracles. There was an older man, Ramon Aponte, who was at the front desk requesting information because his wife was very ill. He wanted to know what he needed to prepare because he had a lot in the cemetery where his mother was buried years ago. I took down his mother's name and date of passing and went up the stairs to the file room to get the information I needed. Since his mother's burial was in 1980, that information was not on the computer. The man sat patiently on a sofa near the exit door as I went to get the file.

I got to the third floor, and the lights were turned off. I had to walk to the back of the room, where the books were, to flip the switch on. It was quiet. I could hear my steps on the wood floor. I went to the burial book first. The pages were very thin and delicate, and they smelled old. Once I located the lot number where the mother had been buried, I placed the book back in its metal drawer and went to my right into the world of files to locate the file. I was startled by a loud thud. A large pile of files was dropped on the floor suddenly. I hadn't touched anything yet... I thought, "*Ofelia?*" or maybe it was in the farthest part, where the shelves are wood and old and might have fallen.

I went over to check and saw Suzy on the second shelf, legs spread open, a jean skirt up to her stomach, and Miguel, pants on the floor, between her legs. The files were all on the floor behind them. Suzy looked up and saw me. Startled, she pushed Miguel off her and

45

began to cover herself. I didn't know how to react. I stopped in my tracks, looked away, and turned around. I began walking down the stairs quickly. As I practically ran down, Tita asked me if I found Don Ramon's file. I went directly to the man sitting on the couch.

I apologized and said it would take me some time to find the information. "I will call you before 5 p.m. with all you need so that you don't have to wait." Ramon was understanding and left. I sat at the extra office chair that was always at reception, even though there was only one employee there.

Tita stared at me. "You ok?'' I hadn't noticed my face was red. I told her to give me a minute to process what I had just seen. She laughed.

"You know there are no secrets in this place... Did Suzy say something to you?"

I didn't know whether to say what I had seen, so I paused. "Nope, nothing." Tita knew I was stopping myself from saying something. We both looked up at the glass door in the entrance and saw a gray Jeep pulling up and honking her horn. It was Gwendolyn. She got out of the car and took her baby out of the car seat. Since there was no response, she honked again. And in a few seconds, her sister Suzy raced down the stairs. I didn't look her in the face as she passed me in a hurry. She went outside, took the baby in her arms, and waited outside. Gwendolyn left in her car. A few minutes passed, and Miguel came down, took his child, and went up the stairs once again. Tita and I watched the scene. Suzy came back in and headed straight to the stairs, following Miguel, without saying a word. Tita looked at me silently and grinned. I kept looking away and did not say a word. We both sat in silence for the rest of the shift.

I called Don Ramon with what he needed before I left that day. Suzy printed the flyers for the next church service she was participating in, using the company printer, as usual, and then left early with some excuse about her back hurting. Miguel came down with his daughter right after Suzy left and said, "Good afternoon, see you Monday," as if we were unable to see the baby in his arm. Tita smiled at me and asked if I had anything else to do that night because she had a lot of paperwork to file and didn't want to be left alone with all the mysterious noises in the file room. Of course, I stayed to help her.

After about an hour, we decided it was enough for the week and went towards the time stamp machine. Just before clocking out, Tita looked up at me with a serious look on her face. "So, when are you going to tell me what happened?" I registered my time stamp and kept silent.

Some things are not worth talking about. Secrets are never permanent situations. I could hear Ofelia humming that song from the third floor at a distance as I walked towards my car in the parking lot.

Chapter 11:

Pigs

ngela stood at the front gate of the cemetery every morning. I noticed when I arrived for work that I was usually about 30 minutes early. She would stand in the middle of the entrance, gates open. She was usually facing the cemetery. That Wednesday, I noticed she was singing. It seemed like a chant, almost. It was in a different language. Not English or Spanish. I parked close to the entrance gates that day and observed her. She had her eyes closed and kept chanting with her closed fists facing down at the sides of her body. She was wearing her work uniform. White, long-sleeved shirt, with a logo sewn on top of her right-side shirt pocket that read "Flamboyán Memorial Park." She never wore her name tag, even though she was supposed to. The shirt was never tucked in, and she usually wore beige trousers. Her shoes were usually colorful. Either orange or yellow. Which was odd because she worked at a cemetery. Jose arrived with his blue BMW and approached the entrance slowly because Angela was standing right at the center of the open gates. He stared at her as he drove by, looked over at me sat in my car, and started to laugh. It was a bullying kind of laughter, for lack of a better way to describe it. I couldn't hear him, but the expression on his face said it all. Right as Jose was parking his car next to mine in reverse, Angela did her final chant, raised both of her closed fists, and opened her hands, throwing up many pennies and what looked like a cloud of chalk. The pennies fell on the ground, and she walked away from the entrance to enter her shift. While observing her, I remembered a conversation I once overheard outside of Miguel's office. Nelson was having an argument with Miguel and saying that he would not touch the money at the entrance—that if he wanted to pick it up, he would have to do it himself. I didn't know what they were talking about until this moment.

Once Angela entered her work shift, she would always take the smallest golf cart and drive around the cemetery in the morning. Nobody really cared or knew why. That day, I was curious enough to observe her. She took a large plastic bag from a box underneath her desk and headed out to the cemetery park for her morning drive. I pretended to head back to my car for something in order to be able to observe what the morning routine consisted of. The 200 strings of property at Flamboyán Memorial Park were surrounded by a cement wall. The lots close to the walls were all small grass memorials. In the center of the cemetery were the larger, cement, above-ground graves.

I noticed Angela drove around the grass area, between the graves, never over them, close to the cement walls all around the cemetery. I stood near my car observing her, at a distance already, and she abruptly stopped. It looked like there were black spots flying in the air where she was. There was something on the ground, and I couldn't quite make out what it was. She took a handkerchief from her shirt pocket and placed it over her mouth and nose with her right hand. She walked over to what was on the ground and placed the black bag on the floor. The black spots were all over her, flying frantically; they were large flies. I stood, trying to see what she placed in the black bag, using her left hand only. It was large, kind of round... It had a face. What? A pig's head! I felt my stomach get sick.

I turned around to walk back to the office and noticed Jose was still in his car. He was on the phone, talking, laughing. No rush to clock in. He was late every day but never said anything about it. He would just have a few laughs with Miguel and talk about how they would have a drink next Friday, and it was all good. He noticed the look on my face and looked up at Angela. She was already closing the black bag. He shrugged, looked back at me, and continued his conversation. As I walked into the office entrance again, I heard the golf cart getting closer. I turned around and saw her drive right past me toward the open entrance gates of the cemetery. She placed the bag on the sidewalk, on the outside of the graveyard, right at the roots of that beautiful blue Flamboyán tree, and headed back toward the office. Sometimes, it's just better not to ask any questions. I sat at my desk and thought about what I had just seen. It is one of the few times in my life where I have questioned what I saw and if I was losing my mind.

Angela sat in her cubicle, humming her usual songs, smiling. I looked blankly at the computer right in front of me, with my hands holding the sides of my face. Disbelief still. Then there was a loud, almost howling sound, and the ground shook suddenly and then stopped. Angela and I looked at each other. Then it shook again, this time without stopping. It felt as if a wave was moving the ground. The wood doors creaked, and I could hear Tita's screaming at the reception near us. I got under my desk as fast as I could and waited with my eyes closed tight. I felt the darkness of my eyelids. The electricity went out, and after what seemed like an endless 50-60 seconds, the ground stopped. I heard steps of people running down the stairs and screaming. I came to my senses and got up as fast as I could. I ran to Tita. She had her head between her knees and was holding it with her hands. She was shaking so much.

"Tita, we have to go outside!" She looked up at me and extended one arm. I helped her up and almost carried her to the exit.

Once outside, we waited, just in case the ground shook again. Jose opened his car door and stood outside. We were all silent for a moment. I took the phone from my right pocket and called my mother. She answered the phone frantically. "Are you ok?" "Yes, ma, are you?" "Virgen Santa, that was an earthquake."

I went straight to my mother's house that day. Mami is the only comfort when the ground shakes. I didn't leave her side until the next day.

Chapter 12:

<u>Trauma</u>

Dissociative amnesia is the concept that explains how some people forget or block out traumatic events from their memory when they have been exposed to difficult, life-changing situations. It's interesting how the brain will protect itself, especially from one's own self. Some days I remember more than others. You can't feel anything if you don't remember—if you force yourself not to think about something, not to say it. Some feelings are just too strong to be described with words. Grief is one of the worst. The word itself is not enough to identify it. The best expression of feelings like those is silence. One can only write in silence… No wonder it is a form of therapy for so many people.

Chapter 13:

<u>Bosses</u>

I once had a boss who would stand in different corners of the building, hiding and listening in on employees' conversations. It was in the marketing firm I got fired from before I worked at the cemetery. She was thin, pale, and black, with thin hair, under her shoulders. Always dressed in office attire, yet never completely neat. The first time I saw her, she moved quickly, and I figured I was mistaken. But then I saw her a second time. I remember asking myself, "*What must go through someone's mind to do something like that?*" In my case, I didn't really care because I usually got my work done and left. I'm not one to have many friends in the workplace. But I couldn't help but ask myself what she expected to find out with that exercise. I never mentioned that to my fellow coworkers. Let things be what they will, I always say.

One day, she was sitting on the floor in the corner of a metal cubicle wall we had. That corner consisted of a small space between the cement wall of the building and the metal wall of the cubicles. Suddenly, we heard her screaming. She discovered she was sitting right next to the entrance of the home of a huge rat, who came out of its spot, not afraid at all of her. He was hairy, had a long tail, and had to be about 5-6 pounds. A huge rat. With her screams, one of my coworkers stood up and saw where she was. It was hilarious to watch her explain what she was doing, sitting there with her work computer. A few days later, she was in the hospital. She had Hantavirus Pulmonary Syndrome, a viral disease spread by rodent droppings. It took her months to recover.

Miguel was much less controlling. To be honest, there was no noticeable difference when he was in his office from when he didn't show up. Except in Suzy's attitude. When he was not there, she was quiet. But when he was, she was loud and outspoken, always fixing her skirt when she stood up from her desk chair. Always looking into a small mirror she had on the right side of her cubicle, fixing her hair. Suzy was not a particularly "pretty" person, and she would usually be rolling her eyes at people or being the office gossip. At one point, when Miguel stopped coming to the office for about a month due to "personal reasons," she decided to try to flirt with Nelson as she would come and go to her vehicle. Nelson would always smile at her yet never spoke too much to her. He would tell Emilio that he did not trust "office people." Nelson also happened to be married, and his wife would bring his lunch to the cemetery almost every day. She came in a red Corolla, rolled down her windshield once at the entrance, gave him his meal, and left in a hurry.

One Tuesday, she arrived just as Suzy was coming back from getting her bag from her car and noticed her smiling at him. Nelson's wife, Becky, had a serious look on her face yet said nothing. She gave him his meal, rolled up her window, and watched as Suzy went back into the office before she made a U-turn at the gate and was on her way out. About an hour later, Tita received a call at the reception desk from a customer asking if Suzy was in on Friday. He needed to know her schedule because he was coming to meet with her about some papers that he could not find. Although it seemed strange that Suzy would be doing anything work-related in that office, Tita looked at the paper schedule that was placed at that desk weekly and told the person, yes, she would be in.

Friday arrived, and it was Tita was off. When it was Tita's day off, someone from the second floor had to fill in for reception that day. Since there was flu going around, there were only two people on that day, and Suzy had to cover the reception desk. There was a line of angry customers at noon, and there was even a lady that was asking where Tita was because this girl was too slow. The stress was getting to Suzy.

Then suddenly, the red Corolla pulled up right in front of the reception doors. Nelson's wife looked in and saw Suzy. The car was left in the middle of the entrance. Nelson's wife got out of the driver's seat, leaving the car door wide open. She was in blue jeans, a white t-shirt, and her hair blow-dried, yet up in a ponytail. She walked right to the entrance in what seemed like three or four steps. She bluntly opened the door, pushed the people in line out of the way, and reached in with her body above the reception desk, grabbing Suzy by the hair with her left hand. Startled, Suzy tried to release her hold from her hair and, with her right hand, punched her right in the mouth. The people in the line were startled by a man trying to pull the woman off of the desk. And another right hook to the mouth. There was blood all over her fist. As the scene progressed, Nelson noticed the car and ran into the office in his muddy boots. "¿¡Que tu haces?!" (What are you doing?!) He was able to grab hold of his wife with enough strength to get her off the desk. He carried her out the door while she continued to yell and swing punches. "¡¡Por putas es que las matan!!" (Whores get killed!!) As she was carried out the door, sirens from a police car could be heard. Nelson was yelling outside, trying to get his wife in the passenger seat. She continued to try to fight him off. Nelson was a big man. Black, tall, about 250 pounds, and she was short, about 120 pounds.

As the police car pulled up, she stopped yelling. The policeman parked his car right behind the Corolla and opened the door to get out of the vehicle. Nelson hurried into the driver's seat, turned on the car, and stepped on the gas. He turned the car right in the entrance and drove right past the police car door, barely making it without crashing. The police officer quickly got in the driver's seat, closed his door, and followed. Most of the customers were already outside, witnessing as the scene took place. Suzy was crying, with her hands on her face as blood came from her mouth, a tooth on the reception desk. One of the customer's called an ambulance, yet an hour passed, and it never arrived. Miguel took Suzy in his car to the nearest hospital. Nelson was never seen at the cemetery again, and Suzy took a leave of absence for some time. About two months later, she resigned because "God had different plans for her."

Chapter 14:

<u>Family</u>

The hearse arrived, and an additional vehicle full of flowers was behind it. The widow was in the front seat of the hearse, accompanied by the funeral attendant. She was visibly affected. Eyes swollen, red. There were no more tears left in her. She was maybe 33 years old, with red hair and a light green blouse. They were at the entrance gate waiting. The cars that accompanied the service were behind them. The first car behind the hearse was a black Lexus SUV with leather interiors. It had belonged to the deceased. The widow's sister drove it to the service so that she could assist in the hearse. The rest of the friends and family members were in their cars, in a line, waiting outside the entrance.

Jose had sold the lot to this family. But, as usual when his clients arrived, he was nowhere near. There was a secluded space, away from the visibility of the street, behind the building where he would stand and smoke a cigarette until someone else had to take care of the family for the service. The routine was that once the family passed the gate, he would mysteriously reappear and go to Miguel's office to ask what had happened to the family and why no one had told him they had arrived. It was the same skit over and over again. They would laugh about it on Fridays while having their weekly beer in the gas station nearby. No big deal.

On this particular day, Angela was the chosen one to take the family to the grave and accompany them while the burial took place. There were over 30 cars, all luxurious. The deceased had five brothers and two sisters. They all seemed older than the widow. One of his brothers said a prayer as the burial took place and said that they had lost the oldest of the eight. As the field workers closed the grave, the widow was standing nearby with her sister, head down, still crying. The rest of the family and friends started heading to their cars and leaving, and the brother who gave the final prayer opened the door to the black SUV, turned the key that had been left in the ignition, and drove away. The hearse also pulled away slowly from the graveside once the grave was closed and the flowers were being placed on the dirt above it.

In front of the grave was the widow, her sister standing by her side with her arm around her, and Angela in the golf cart, waiting. As the widow turned to her, Angela asked her, "Should I drive you back to the office?" Her sister immediately turned and looked around.

"The car was stolen!" she yelled. The widow finally looked up and around and started to cry again.

Angela, with a confused look still on her face, tried to calm them down and said, "His brother just drove off in the car. I saw him. Did he have the key?" The widow then realized she knew what was going on.

Her sister was still yelling, "How can this be? Why didn't anyone stop him?"

The widow, still crying silently, told Angela in a low, almost broken voice, "Please take us to the office." She did.

There was only one family at the cemetery that day, and Jose was already selling them the lot for their service. Angela sat with the widow and her sister and listened to the story as they waited for a taxi. Beth (the widow) had been living with Luis (the deceased) for the past 15 years. They were happy and very much in love. Luis was 40 years older than Beth. He was wealthy, and they lived a good life together. During his sickness, she took care of him until he passed, which was his wish. Luis' family did not agree with their relationship due to the age difference. Beth never thought it was necessary to get married because they lived their love day by day. Beth's sister called the brother to question his actions, to which he replied, "Luis is dead, and we are the heirs. Beth no longer has any say in any of his belongings." Beth kept talking and crying as the events progressed. She was in disbelief at what was happening. Angela waved goodbye as they both left in a taxi and recited a prayer to provide them strength for the days to come.

About a week later, Angela saw Beth visiting Luis' grave. She was picking up some of the dead flowers that were left and placing some pictures of them on the ground. She stopped the golf cart to say hello, and Beth gave her an update. She was now homeless. Luis' family members changed the locks on what had been her home for 15 years, and she had to get a lawyer to start the legal process to obtain her belongings. She was left with nothing. The joint bank account, with the funds frozen until the declaration of heirs, was made. Beth looked at Angela with sadness and disappointment in her eyes. "I didn't think to get married. I didn't want it to look like I was a gold digger." Angela drove back to the office and told me what had happened.

"La gente es mala. Never trust, kid," she told me. Reality can be harsh sometimes.

Chapter 15:

Blue Flowers

The Blue Flamboyán, also known as Jacaranda, is native to the North of Argentina in South America. It grows quickly, 25 to up to 40 feet high in Puerto Rico. It is rare and most seen in the town of Cidra, which is not far from Caguas. The flowers are like small trumpets. The colors are blue or purple. Its real beauty is hidden for most of the year, and then it will surprise you from April to May when you can see it full of flowers. The Blue Flamboyán in front of Flamboyán Memorial Park was rare. It only flourished the first week of April of each year. Then the flowers would slowly fall out, making the ground around it look like a blue carpet. Sometimes, I would sit under that tree during my lunch break to pass the time. It was nice and peaceful compared to the chaos that was always around us at that cemetery office. Emilio would always observe the tree as he drove in and out of the cemetery. Emilio didn't speak much. But his eyes spoke.

After eating, I would enjoy laying on the roots of the Flamboyán and looking up. Parts of the sky could be seen between the leaves. I felt at ease in that spot. It was a beautiful feeling. The sound of birds chirping, the wind kindly caressing my hair and face. Although the tree was in front of the cemetery, just beside the road, there was not much traffic in the area. A car would pass every now and then, usually speeding by. When there was a service, there would be a funeral hearse arriving, and cars of family members and friends would slowly follow.

In Puerto Rico, it was common to have a vehicle in front of the funeral hearse that had a large speaker playing either the music that the deceased heard or gospel music. Some families would even make matching t-shirts with the photo of the person who passed away on them. As a culture, we have a particular way of dealing with grief and trauma, and it's usually a celebration. Even in the worst moments, we sing and dance. These are the things I took time to notice when time stood still for me under that Blue Flamboyán. Things nobody thinks about, or at least nobody talks about. I grew to love that spot.

Chapter 16:

<u>Mental Health</u>

There comes a time when you stop wondering who it is you are and know for certain. It's a moment in time when you question everything that you once were or believed true. You must have experienced it at some point. That instant where you are unsure of what the Hell it is you are doing. You can't tell the difference between good and bad anymore. You question every aspect of yourself, including your morals and your beliefs. Although some think of this moment as insane, in my case, I would say it's the only moment where I've felt sanity. Where I've been able to hear my own breathing, to stop thinking, to just exist, maybe even stop caring for a few eternal seconds. Stop trying to control. To enjoy that emotion or the lack of it. Just stopping gives an immense sense of relief. You've been in survival mode so long it's even uncomfortable to stop. But it's in that moment where you decide if the voice is actually in your brain or you accept that you are being spoken to; you decide whether to listen on that particular day to yourself or whoever speaks inside of you. You realize that that weight you felt on your shoulders... was a loss of yourself. You start to remember the list of things you once enjoyed, your talents, and the things that drive you and make you unique. You start drawing the things you did in high school or grade school, when life was much simpler, when you still had not dealt with chaos, grief, and people... Then life starts to make so much more sense again. You begin to live again. Turns out it's not the same thing to be alive as to be living. For some, it takes true trauma to get to that point: surviving a major illness, an abusive relationship, results of impulsive decision-making. Then life begins. And you never look back.

It takes years of therapy to be able to let go as described. The average person has no idea how burdening it is to work at a place like a cemetery.

Chapter 17:

<u>Chico</u>

A lot of people visit gravesides at a cemetery. I did not believe so until I saw it with my own eyes. Emilio was always the first person to arrive at the cemetery, usually around 6:30 a.m. every day. He had the gate keys, so he would always leave one gate open while he sat inside his parked car to eat his breakfast and have his coffee. At 8 a.m., when the office opened, we would always see people visiting their family members' gravesides early in the morning. Some people would see it daily. That Wednesday, a very old woman that lived in a small home made of wood nearby drove in right after Emilio opened the gate. She parked next to him. She was about 90 years old, with white hair and swollen eyes. She was crying. She knew Emilio; she was his neighbor. The old woman lived in her house alone with a black Chao Chao named Chico. He was an old dog, about 14 years old. His face was covered in gray hair, and he had a cancerous tumor in his neck. Mercy was a poor woman;

she had no means to take Chico to the vet, so she decided to let nature take its course. Chico died while sleeping that morning. Mercy wrapped him in a used bed sheet and dragged and placed Chico in the back seat of her 2000 Mitsubishi Mirage. She begged Emilio to help her bury Chico. She had no means to cremate him, and besides her car and the little belongings in her home, she only had a cement grave at the cemetery.

During the years when Puerto Rico was a Spanish Colony, cement graves became very common on the island. It was also common for people to have their burials inside single niches that looked like drawers inside church walls or underneath the temple. For larger family graves, they made above-ground concrete chambers. It was a large cement container with shelves on the inside. There were graves that could fit from 3 to 10 caskets inside each. Above the shelves was an opening in the chamber with a large concrete plate over it. This plate would be removed by cemetery personnel for the placing of a deceased family member inside the grave. On the outside, it could have cement decorations (for the poor) or granite (for the wealthier families). It was also common for people to have statues of Jesus or the Virgin Mary praying over their loved ones and flowers.

Mercy was twice a widow, and both husbands were buried in her cement grave at Flamboyán Memorial Park. When Emilio looked in the back seat and saw that Chico was in the sheets, he did not even say a word. He left his half-eaten sandwich in his car and told Mercy to sit in the passenger seat as he drove her Mirage to the large cement grave she had almost at the back of that huge cemetery. There was a storage area nearby where he got a ladder to place inside the large cement chamber once he moved the concrete plate over the grave. He carefully took Chico's body, over his shoulder, down that ladder. It was impressive how strong Emilio was. Once at the end, he yelled at Mercy, "¿En cual tablilla?" (On which shelf?) Mercy, still crying, looked in the chamber and said, "En la segunda, con Pito" (In the second one, with Pito). Pito was Mercy's second husband. He had adopted Chico when he was a puppy at a local rescue center. Once Pito died, Chico began to fall ill. Once Mercy saw Emilio climbing back up the ladder, she sighed in relief. "Gracias, gracias!" as she hugged him. Emilio placed the lid on the grave and drove back to his car. It was still 15 minutes before 7:30 a.m., and no one else had arrived at the cemetery.

Chapter 18:

<u>Sleeping</u>

The funeral parlors on the island were supposed to be open 24 hours a day. In the evening shift, there was usually one person left at the funeral home to attend to any calls that were received to pick up deceased remains at night. These calls were usually made by hospital personnel or family members of people who were under hospice care in their homes and passed away. It was usual for the front door to be locked. In the funeral parlor that was closest to Flamboyán Memorial Park, it was always Fernando covering the evening to the next morning shift. It was from 9:00 p.m. – 5:00 a.m., six days a week. Sundays were the only evenings in which there was no one at the funeral home at night. Fernando was an odd man. He was 26 years old and about 5' 3" tall. Black, curly hair, almost covering his eyes like a curtain. He rarely looked anyone in the eyes. Very quiet. Others only knew he spoke because he picked up the phone to receive calls at the funeral home. It was also the only time one could observe a subtle smile on his face. His tone was always very professional, and his voice had a rare depth to it. He was thin, maybe 100 pounds. Pale skin. He always wore black, long-sleeved shirts, sometimes a black sweater on top, and black shoes with platforms. Around his neck, he always wore a necklace with spikes and silver rings on each of the fingers of his hands. He was a peculiar man.

The funeral home's manager, Katherine, began to receive complaints because no one would answer the phone some evenings. Fernando was always disciplined with his timestamps and was rarely absent from work. There were no cameras in the funeral home. Katherine asked Fernando about the complaints, and he never responded. His stare was focused on the wall behind her. She decided to take matters into her own hands and investigate.

On a random Tuesday evening, Katherine went to the funeral home at midnight to check on Fernando. The front door was locked, as usual, because there was no one else there, and no families were visiting at night. It was glass, so you could see into the parlor. She knocked on the glass, no response. She looked through the door and saw no movement through the building. The reception desk was empty, and all of the rooms where the viewings were held had their doors open, except for the one to the far left. Before getting the key from her right pocket to open the glass door, Katherine decided to go around the building to check where the funeral vehicles were parked, just in case Fernando was there. Nothing. Just silence and the squeak of the bats that loved hunting insects at that time of night.

Katherine went back to the front door. She got the key from her right pocket and opened it, trying to be as silent as possible. Locked the door behind her. The lights were dim. She walked past the open doors and saw nobody. Then she arrived at the only closed door. It was the largest viewing room in the building. Outside, there was the name of the deceased that would be placed the next day. She slowly turned the knob on the wood door and opened it.

The room was dark, and it took a few seconds for her vision to adapt. Then, she could see the large room empty, flowers placed for the service the next day, casket closed. She took a few moments to walk around and inspect and turn on the lights. It was strange that the casket had already been placed in the viewing room. That part was usually done in the mornings. She walked over to take a look and got startled as she touched the side clips to open the casket. Someone or something was pushing to open the casket from the inside. Katherine stepped back and shut her eyes; her hand automatically went to cover them. She could hear someone sitting up in the coffin in front of her. She mustered up the courage to look up through her hand covering her face. It was Fernando sitting up in the casket. Katherine stepped back once again. "What the hell are you doing in there?" He gave her his same blank stare and said nothing. He just laid back in the coffin and closed it. Katherine, still scared and confused, went toward the door and turned off the lights. She closed the door and left the funeral home as found. The incident was never spoken of. She never explained to the customers why the phone was not answered after a certain hour. No one would believe what she just saw. To be honest, neither did she.

Chapter 19:

Rain

Rain came daily in the mountains. On some days, it seemed like the only raincloud was right above Flamboyán Memorial Park, and everywhere else was sunny. It was usually a pattern of brief heavy rainfall, and then it stopped for a few hours, and then it would rain again. I used to love the rain. The only issue with the weather was when there was a burial taking place. The cement properties would quickly fill up with water, and the grass properties would become this thick, red mud. Even boots and raincoats did not protect the field workers from sliding in the mud as they placed the caskets and tried to close the lots as quickly as possible. It was not a pretty sight. Sometimes the mud slid into the grave with the rainfall as they placed the casket inside the burial space. There was usually a vault in the ground, cement or bronze, depending on what the family had paid for, and the casket was placed inside.

When it was raining, sometimes the vault would be filled with water and mud. Affected family members would cry and scream that there was mud on their loved ones. The field workers never flinched and never stopped to look at the distressed family. They had to get the job done, and they did. Afterward, it was our job at the office to console the family, to explain we had no control over the weather and that there was no other way to go about it.

Now I feel sadness when it rains. The sound of the rain brings mud and loss to my mind. I can't shake the memories left by Hurricane Maria when the rain killed so many people. 4,645, and it's not an accurate figure. Loss. Theirs and mine. The circumstances change, but the feeling is the same. I know exactly how hopeless they feel.

Chapter 20:

What goes up...

It was a good day. There were a group of small, green parrots in one of the trees inside the cemetery that day. It was a Cupey tree they loved. They had different colors in the feathers underneath their wings, and you could see as they flapped to hold on to the branches and munched at the leaves and fruits of the tree. They were usually loud; it almost looked like they were having an argument or a funny conversation amongst themselves. It is a sight that brings color and warmth to the heart, even inside a place like a cemetery. The weather was also beautiful, and it was a sunny day. No rainclouds in sight, finally. It had been raining every day for three weeks straight. Even though there was no rain, you could still feel the water in the ground as it was stepped on.

There were only two field workers that came to work that day. Many had suffered back injuries from the burials done in the weeks prior. Emilio was one present, so I knew that the burials on that sunny day, at least, would run smoothly. I was a bit anxious. We were expecting a very large service that day. I knew that Jose would do his usual bit and hide, so I was prepared. I went into the office, finished some paperwork I had on my desk, took it up to the administration workers, and disappeared just ten minutes before I knew the service would arrive. I told Tita my plan, and she did the same. Suddenly, Tita was nowhere to be found, and the reception desk was empty. I was in one of the bathrooms, and Tita was on her way to the parking lot to get something from her car.

Once the service was at their grave, we would meet under the Blue Flamboyán and take our breaks at the same time to sit and chat for a while. Angela was sick that day and did not come to work. Administration workers rarely left the second floor. Miguel had no other option but to tell Jose to take the funeral vehicle to the property. It was a very large service. By the hearse were three motorcycles. One was burning rubber in a circular motion as Jose and Miguel got the golf cart to lead them to the burial site. There were young men on the motorcycles, 20 years old at the most. The two that were by the funeral vehicle were thin and serious, staring directly at the front. On their back, each had a sling that held a large rifle. As they went by the gates, there was loud music, people with the car windows open and sitting on the edges of the doors, holding onto the car roofs. You could not hear yourself think. Most of them had white t-shirts and a picture of the loved one that had passed. He was about the same age as the men on the motorcycles. Traffic was stopped on the road leading to the cemetery. There were over sixty cars following for the service. All had noise and music; there was smoke all over. The smell of burning rubber immersed everything around it. Following the funeral hearse was a black Honda Accord with its windows up. They were the only ones with no music. A large black man wearing a gray suit drove, and to his side was an older woman, holding a picture of the deceased to her chest tight. She had her eyes closed and her head facing down. She was his grandmother.

Jose took the motorcycles and funeral hearse straight to the burial spot, which was in the center of the cemetery, the cement, above-ground tombs. He seemed like he was racing toward the property. Once there, he gave instructions to quickly place the casket above the wood planks placed on the open grave. The grandmother took her time to walk over; the large man that was driving was her church's pastor. The rest of the people who accompanied them let the old lady walk by as they went to the grave also. Some carried opened bottles of rum and beer cans. The armed young men that escorted the service stood about 12 feet from where the service was taking place, dark sunglasses on, just observing in silence. One of them was smoking as he watched over the crowd. Before Jose knew it, he was surrounded by the crowd. The grandmother was right in front of her grandson's casket. People were talking, crying, screaming, just chaos all around... and then she looked up and yelled, "¡¡Silencio!!" It took two seconds to have automatic silence. Even the cemetery employees stopped in their tracks. Then she looked over to her pastor, and he began his prayer.

Once the pastor gave the blessing, the field workers began to place the casket in the cement lot. As they descended, shots were fired into the air from the rifles of the young men watching the service from afar. The chaos continued as cries and screams were being heard from the people at the service. The grandmother stood in front of the grave until the workers finished. She cried in silence, and the pastor had his arm around her. She turned to her right to begin walking down the cement path to the car she came in. The people made room for her to go by. Before the grave was closed, some got close and poured their beers and rum inside.

As the burial took place, it took me a while to get outside to meet Tita. Many cars were parked in the way, and two families had come into the office on foot and caught me right as I was leaving the bathroom. I quickly took care of their matters and went to meet Tita outside as planned. She was lying under the Blue Flamboyán, looking up at the leaves. It was April 3rd, so the flowers were gorgeous. The wind blew, and I could see some of the flowers falling on Tita, yet she didn't move. As I came closer, I saw Tita wasn't moving. "Girl, this is no time for a nap!" I said while laughing. When I looked over at Tita, her head lying on the Blue Flamboyán roots, I saw something dark above her left eye. There was blood all over the roots and on the side of her face. I couldn't breathe. I got down on my knees and pushed at her chest, listened... Nothing. She was dead. She had been shot. As I ran back to the office to call for help, the motorcycles escorting the service that afternoon went racing by me. The breeze kept throwing flowers at Tita's lifeless body. Her notebook of names had fallen next to her right hand, right beside her. Pages turned as the wind blew.

It's an immense sense of relief to no longer work at that cemetery, like a burden that has been lifted. I do miss sitting beneath that Blue Flamboyán, though. I still drive by slowly from time to time just to look at it. I stop to feel the breeze for a moment when it's not raining. A smile takes over my face as I close my eyes and remember Tita's jokes and crazy stories. As I look at those cemetery gates after those moments, I can't help but wonder how many other stories still lie behind those old gates... I wonder if anyone will ever tell them.

Printed in Great Britain
by Amazon

21896811R00047